Love

THE SELFISH GIANT

Adapted by Janet Quinlan

Illustrated by Sherry Neidigh

8 7 6 5 4 3 2 1
ISBN 1-4127-3758-3

Once there was a giant who lived in a large castle near the center of town. It was a very fine castle, yet the giant was seldom at home to enjoy it. Instead, he spent many years traveling restlessly from place to place.

While the giant was away, the children of the town came to play in his garden each day after school. It was the most beautiful garden in the land, and some said it was enchanted.

Inside the garden it was summer all year long. The trees never lost their leaves, the flowers were always in bloom, and the weather never got cold. Sometimes it rained, but only at night when the children were asleep in their beds. It was always sunny again in the morning.

The children skipped rope, swung from the trees, and played games in the enchanted garden. When they grew hungry, they plucked fruit from the trees and ate it. The children were very happy in the garden.

One day, the giant returned home. He had grown weary during his travels and longed for the peace and quiet of his castle.

Instead, loud noises greeted him when he arrived. He heard happy shouts and sounds of laughter. When he looked out the window, he saw children playing games and eating fruit from the trees in his garden.

"What are you children doing here?" bellowed the giant. "This is my garden! I will allow no one to play here but myself." The children were very frightened and ran away as fast as their legs could carry them.

With that, the giant placed a heavy lock on the gate to the garden. He also hung a wooden sign on the garden wall, announcing that no one was allowed to enter. This satisfied the giant.

"Finally," he growled to himself, "I will have some peace and quiet."

He was a very selfish giant.

Now the children no longer had a place to play. They would walk sadly past the garden on their way home from school and remember the fun they once had there. One day, they stopped by the gate. A curious boy wanted to see the garden, so he climbed on top of his friend's shoulders and peeked over the wall.

The boy gasped at what he saw. The leaves of the trees were turning orange and falling to the ground. The grass was now thin and brown. The flowers had wilted, and the tree branches drooped.

"What has happened to our wonderful garden? It looks like it is dying," said the boy. The children were miserable. A few even began to cry. Their beautiful garden was no longer enchanted.

The garden had become a very cold and lonely place. The birds had fled, and the only sound that could be heard was the mournful cry of the cold wind as it blew through the empty tree branches.

One day, a lovely red flower poked its head out of the ground. The giant noticed it from his window and hoped it would grow tall and strong. Instead, a gust of wind roared through the garden and scared the little flower back underground.

The giant sighed. He did not understand what was happening to his garden. It had once been so beautiful, but now it was dull and cold.

"Well," sighed the giant, "at least now I have peace and quiet. And I do not have to share my garden with anyone."

These thoughts made the giant feel better. He truly was a selfish giant.

The passing months brought even more changes to the garden. Stinging white snow swirled in the wind, and sharp icicles hung from the trees. Nobody would have played in the frozen garden, even if the giant had invited them inside.

The giant was puzzled. He could see that it was no longer winter in the rest of the countryside. The weather had turned warm and sunny, and new green shoots were springing up everywhere. Why, then, was it still so bleak in his garden?

"Something is not right," the giant said. He began to wish for his beautiful garden and for the children who had made it such a happy place. For the first time, the giant felt lonely.

The children continued to stop by the gate after school, wishing they could play in the green garden they remembered. One day, a loose stone fell out of the wall. The hole it left was big enough for the children to crawl through. They looked at each other excitedly and entered the secret passage, one by one.

The children knew that if the giant found them in his garden, he would be furious. But they missed the garden too much to stay away.

Then something incredible happened. When their feet touched the ground, the snow began to melt. The grass turned green, and the sun began to shine. When the children climbed and swung from the trees, new leaves appeared on the branches.

From inside the castle, the giant heard a bird singing. Amazed, he went to the window. What was happening? The garden was coming back to life! The giant's eyes filled with tears. "How selfish I have been," he said, shaking his head. He was very sorry for what he had done.

Icicles still hung from one tree. A small boy looked up at the tree sadly. He wanted to climb it, but he could not reach even the lowest branch.

The boy sat down under the tree and began to cry.

Suddenly, he felt a huge pair of hands gently lift him up and set him on a branch. Instantly, the icicles melted. They were replaced by fresh green leaves.

The surprised little boy turned to see the giant who had once roared with anger at the children. Now the giant smiled and patted the little boy on the head.

The boy flung his arms around the giant's neck and kissed him on the cheek. The giant's heart melted as quickly as the icicles. He was sorry he had been so selfish. Now he realized how much he had missed the children.

When the other children saw that they no longer had to fear the giant, they rushed over to him. The giant scooped them up and gave them each a giant-sized hug.

It was wonderful to hear the children laugh again.

"Does this mean that we may play in your enchanted garden?" asked one child.

The giant now realized that the children brought the magic to his garden. "From now on this is your garden," the giant said. "You may come here to play whenever you wish."

Love

In this story, the children teach the giant how to love. When the giant decides to lock his garden, he acts selfishly. He wants to be the only one who can enjoy it. But soon the garden turns cold and wintry. The giant realizes that it was the children's love that had made it beautiful. When the children return to the garden and bring it back to life, the giant lets love into his heart. The children show the giant that sharing his garden increases its beauty for everyone.